هدية لبيتر

A Present
For Peter

MANTRA

Text copyright © Bernard Ashley 1996
Illustrations copyright © David Mitchell 1996
Dual language text copyright © Mantra Publishing Ltd 1997
The author/illustrator asserts the moral right to be
identified as the author/illustrator of this Work.

Published by arrangement with HarperCollins Publishers Ltd in 1996
All Rights Reserved

Printed in Hong Kong by South China Printing Co (1988) Ltd

Published by
Mantra Publishing Ltd
5 Alexandra Grove
London N12 8NU
http://www.mantrapublishing.com

هدية لبيتز

A Present
For Peter

BERNARD ASHLEY   **DAVID MITCHELL**

Arabic Translation by Azza Habashi

كان يوم السبت . وكان الرضيع بيتر يتألم بشدة بسبب ظهور سِنة
جديدة له.

It was Saturday and baby Peter was hurting badly with a new
tooth coming through.

قال والد بليجر إنه سيذهب للتسوق وسيأخذ إبنته الكبرى. "من الأفضل أن تبقين عن قرب" قائلاً لها: "إن السوق مزدحمٌ جداً اليوم".

Pleasure's dad said he'd do the shopping at the market and take his big girl. "But you'd better stay close," he told her. "The market is a busy place today."

من أعلى الحافلة، بدا السوق ممتعاً جداً وكأنه معرضاً. قالت بليجر:
"معي جنيه لشراء هدية لبيتر." بينما كان أبوها مشغولاً بمراجعة قائمة
المشتروات.

From the top of the bus the market looked good fun like a fair.
"I have a pound for a present for Peter," Pleasure said. But her
dad was busy checking his list.

بدا السوق مليئاً بأكياس البضائع وكان الأب ومايشغله من مشتروات
كثيرة ممسكاً بيدها بشدة. إشترى من الفلفل و البطاطس والبقول، وبليجر
تحملق في اللعب تريد أن تشتري لعبة لبيتر.

It was all bustle and bags at the market. And Dad with all that shopping
to do. Holding her tightly he bought chillies, potatoes and beans. Pleasure
was eyeing the toys, wanting to get something for Peter.

قال الأب: "سمكا طازج" وترك بليجر تختار. لكنها لم تعطي لذلك إهتماماً شديداً. فإن بيتر لا يريد سمك ولكنه يريد لعبة.

"Fresh fish," Dad said, letting Pleasure choose. But she didn't give it too much of a look. Peter wouldn't want haddock, but he'd like a rattle.

وعندما تركها الأب ليدفع النقود، ذهبت يدها في الحال إلى جيبها، لإنها

شاهدت عضاضة مناسبة تماماً للرضيع ليعض عليها.

When Dad let go to pay, her hand went straight into her pocket.
Because over there was a teething ring - just right for the baby to bite.

إلتفتت إلى والدها باسمة، وهي تفكر كم سيكون بيتر سعيداً باللعبة ـ
ولكن سرعان ما إختفت إبتسامتها في لحظة.
"أبي....!"

She twisted round smiling to tell Dad. She was thinking how
pleased Peter would be - but the smile was wiped off in a flash.
"Dad…!"

كان والدها قد ذهب! فهو لم يكن هناك؟ كيف يكون قد ذهب
بهذه السرعة؟ ونظرت حولها ولكنها لم ترَ إلا أرجل ومعاطف
وحقائب ناسٍ غرباءٍ عنها.

Her dad had gone! *He wasn't there?* Where was he?
How could he have gone so quick? She looked - but all she
could see were strangers' legs and their coats and their bags.

الكل كان هناك، ولكن لا أثر لوالدها! إنقلبت معدتها رأساً على عقب
ـ لقد كان دائماً يقول أنها إبنته الكبيرة، لذلك فهى سوف لا تستسلم
للخوف.

There was everyone else, but no sign of him! Her stomach did a
head over heels - he always said she was his big girl, so she wasn't
going to get scared!

ودفعت بنفسها بين أرجل الناس وشبَّت على أطراف قدميها تفكر أن

أباها لم يذهب بعيداً.

She pushed through legs, she stood on her toes. He couldn't be far.

ونظرت إلى بائع الأشياء المستعملة. وهناك لمحت أباها! لقد كانت محقة.

She looked at the second hand stall. There he was! She was right.

وجرت خلال الزحام...

She ran through the crowd...

... وجذبته من ملابسه بشدة.

... and grabbed hard at his tracksuit.

ولكن الملابس كانت مختلفة وكذلك الوجة.

But the striping was different and so was the face.

الأن فقط شعرت بليجر بالخوف، وكأنها طفلة بمفردها في العالم.

Now Pleasure *did* feel frightened, like the only child in the world.

قال شخص: "إنها تائهة. هذه المسكينة الصغيرة."

"She's lost!" someone said. "The poor little mite!"

ولفتها حلقة من المحملقين،

A whole staring ring of them crowding her in,

كأنهم يلتفون حول طائرٍ جريح.

like trapping a wounded bird.

إلتفتت وجرت إلى حيث لا
تدري ولكن بعيداً عن
أيديهم وصراخهم.
لابد أن يكون في مكانٍ ما!

She turned and ran, she
didn't know where, but
away from their hands
and their shouts. He'd got
to be somewhere!

صاحت: "أبي!" وصارت تعدو خلال السوق...

She shouted, "DAD!" and chased through the stalls...

بين الفساتين المعروضة والفواكه والزهور والحقائب.

...through dresses and fruit and flowers and bags.

حتى وجدت نفسها تصرخ بلهفة عند آخر دكان في السوق، وكان
بائع السمك ـ حيث كان أبوها يراجع نقوده. "ماذا بك يا بنت؟"
فهو لم يفتقدها قَطْ.

Till she came shouting in panic round one last stall, to the fish -
where he was counting his change.
"What's the matter with you, girl?"
He hadn't missed her at all.

فجذبته بشدة تحسباً أن تفقده

مرةً أخرى.

She grabbed him
in case she lost
him again.

وقالت باكيةَ: "أين كنت يا أبي؟".

"أين كنت؟ أنا لم أتحرك شبراً."

"Where were you?" she cried.
"Where was I? I haven't budged an inch."

ثم بدأ يتحدث إليها برقة ليطمئنها.

"هل إخترتِ هدية لبيتر قبل أن أتوه عن بصرك؟"

He then spoke softly to calm her down.
"Did you choose a present for Peter before you lost sight of me?"

وهزت بليجر رأسها عندما رأتها من بين دموعها المتساقطة.

وقالت لوالدها: "العضاضة..."

Pleasure nodded her head and through her tears she saw it.
"The...teething...ring," she told him.

قال الوالد ملاطفاً: "هذا جميل . ولكن ماذا لو إشتريت لك شيئاً

يفرحك بعد ما أصابك من خوف؟"

"That's nice. And what about something for a bit of comfort after a scare?" he said wanting to give her a treat.

.

نظرت بليجر مرة أخرى للسوق، ولكن ليس بشعور إبنته الكبيرة.

قالت: " أريد عروسة،" "ولكن من الأفضل أن نشتري هذه البزازة للرضيع!"

Pleasure looked at the stall again, not feeling like his big girl.
"I'd like a doll," she said, "but I'd better have that babies' dummy!"

وبإبتسامته بدا كل شيئ على ما يرام.

And his smile made everything right.